T0063395

S THE D
ECON
HARVEST

S THE D
SECOND
HARVEST

40 short stories to inspire your self-improvement

NABIL N. JAMAL, PhD

PARTRIDGE
A Penguin Random House Company

Copyright © 2014 by Nabil N. Jamal, PhD.

ISBN: Hardcover   978-1-4828-9678-7
             Softcover   978-1-4828-9677-0
             eBook   978-1-4828-9679-4

All rights reserved. No part of this book may be used or reproduced by any means, graphic, electronic, or mechanical, including photocopying, recording, taping or by any information storage retrieval system without the written permission of the publisher except in the case of brief quotations embodied in critical articles and reviews.

Because of the dynamic nature of the Internet, any web addresses or links contained in this book may have changed since publication and may no longer be valid. The views expressed in this work are solely those of the author and do not necessarily reflect the views of the publisher, and the publisher hereby disclaims any responsibility for them.

To order additional copies of this book, contact
Toll Free 800 101 2657 (Singapore)
Toll Free 1 800 81 7340 (Malaysia)
orders.singapore@partridgepublishing.com

www.partridgepublishing.com/singapore

CONTENTS

Introduction

'*The Second Harvest*' is the sequel to '*A Harvest of Change*', both of which are self-improvement books of forty short stories each, intended to help the reader see that things can be done differently, positively and creatively, to embrace change, and not give up in spite of all the negative influences that surround us.

The sources that I used in researching the stories are: the internet, books, audio recordings, video recordings by renowned authors and speakers, even cartoons, and of course my very own material, all of which are credited at the beginning of each.

Being a performance development facilitator by profession with extensive experience in the field, I use many of those short stories in my sessions to deliver the desired performance changes in participants, very successfully.

People love short stories and associate with them, and a lesson can be better accepted if it is derived from a story; and as such, I believe that anyone, 18 years and above will enjoy reading this book and find benefit in the process.

Acknowledgements

I would like to thank the following people who have helped bring my two books into fruition.

Publisher's Assistant: I would like to start by thanking *Shelly Edmunds* (Publishing Service Associate) at Partridge Publishing, who has helped my two books move very smoothly from one phase to another throughout the publishing process.

Artwork: I would also like to thank the artists who participated in hand-drawing the sketches that you see in my two books, '*A Harvest of Change*' and '*The Second Harvest*'; namely, *Nancy El-Fata*, fifty sketches; *Yvette Ohanian*, twenty nine sketches; *Ali Callanta*, one sketch, and my brother, *Sany Jamal*, one sketch. All other images were made by me.

A very special word of thanks goes to my lovely family members and friends whose varied opinions and input helped me shape the final design for this book's cover.

Finally, to *my family* who has adopted my positive habits, I thank you all for the unwavering group momentum that kept me going until I finished both books.

No Toothpaste

Source: *The internet*

A toothpaste company received complaints from several retailers that the company had been shipping out a few empty toothpaste boxes along with the good ones.

Management instantly pinpointed the problem to that section of the assembly line that transports the packaged toothpaste boxes to the delivery department. The company then installed high-tech precision scales that would sound a bell and flash a light whenever a toothpaste box weighed less than it should; the conveyor belt would also stop, and someone had to walk over and yank the defective box out of line, and press a button when done. This equipment cost several million dollars to install.

At first, the production report showed that the number of empty boxes picked up by the high-tech scales was at least a dozen a day; then suddenly, after three weeks it became Zero! And continued to report Zero for several weeks. The CEO thought that there was something wrong with the report, and so, he visited the factory and walked up to that part of the assembly line where the precision scales were installed. A few feet before it, there was a $20 desk fan, blowing empty boxes out of the belt and into a garbage bin. When asked, one worker replied, "Oh that! Well one of the guys put it there 'cause he was tired of walking over every time the bell rang to remove an empty box".

The worker's solution was both simple and practical. Had Management known about it, they could have saved the millions they spent on the high-tech precision scale system.

The Takeaway: History has thousands of similar incidents where a simple solution solved a big problem. And yet, we tend to assume that for a big problem there must be an expensive solution.

Making it a point to first ask all parties involved in the matter (here, the production line) to give their input for a solution, may save a lot of time and money.

Rowling's Potter

Source: *Wikipedia and other sources on the internet*

J.K. Rowling, author of the famous *Harry Potter* stories and movies, spoke to the graduating class of Harvard in June 2008. She did not talk about success, but rather about failure, her own in particular.

"You might never fail on the scale that I did", Rowling told that privileged audience, *"but it is impossible to live without failing at something, unless you live so cautiously that you might as well not have lived at all - in which case, you fail by default."*

She should know; Rowling did not magically become the 10th richest woman in the world overnight.

Penniless, recently divorced, and raising a child all alone, she wrote the first Harry Potter book in sections in coffee shops, then typed the manuscript on an old manual typewriter.

Twelve (12) publishers rejected her manuscript; but a year later, she was given the green light, and a £1500 advance by the editor from Bloomsbury, a publishing house in London.

The decision to publish Rowling's book apparently owes much to the eight-year-old daughter of Bloomsbury's chairman; her father had given her the first chapter to review, and soon after, she demanded the next.

Although Bloomsbury agreed to publish the book, the editor says he had advised Rowling to get a day job, since she had little chance of making money in children's books.

From then on it was history.

The Takeaway: *What if J.K. gave up after her first rejection, the fifth, the tenth?*

Success can be measured by how many times someone keeps on trying, persisting against negative views of people that matter to the subject (in this case 12 publishers).

"If we don't know failure, how can we know success?"

- Nabil N. Jamal

Space Pen

Source: *The internet*

When NASA began launching astronauts into space in the 1960s, they discovered that their pens did not work at zero gravity (ink wouldn't flow to the writing surface).

It cost NASA over $1 million in research trying to solve this problem. When Paul Fisher developed the "Space Pen" for NASA, it worked at zero gravity, upside down, underwater, on practically any surface including crystals, and in temperature ranges from below freezing to over 300 degrees Celsius.

And what did the Soviets do? They simply used a pencil.

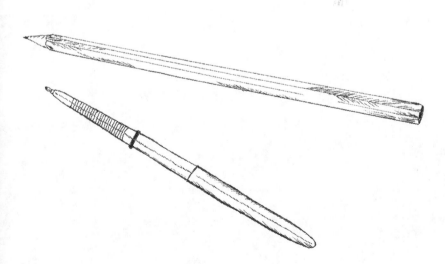

The Takeaway: *This is another case of focusing on the problem and not on the solution. Again because of the importance of the problem, we tend to assume that its solution should be costly.*

Like in the "No Toothpaste" story in this book, sometimes a solution is so simple that we may overlook it.

Colorblindness? No More!

Source: *Facebook*

One out of every ten people has some form of colorblindness.

In 2003, *Mark Changizi*, a neurobiologist and *Tim Barber*, a theoretical computer scientist, were researching means to view changes in skin color.

Their use of filter glasses was originally intended for medical personnel, who could now see blood vessels dilating beneath the skin. The glasses enhanced the contrast between the skin and the blood vessels.

In 2010, they developed the *"O2 Amp"* glasses, which isolates and enhances the red-green part of the spectrum, and *by chance*, these glasses were the solution to colorblindness.

The *02 Amps* were *not intended* as a *fix* for colorblindness, but while Changizi and Barber were showing the glasses to individuals around the world, they found that certain people with colorblindness could now see colors they were otherwise unable to see.

However, inventing is one thing, and selling is another. Barber and Changizi embarked on a *two-year* odyssey to find a manufacturer to make the eyewear that would enable them to sell commercially; until finally, in 2012, they found a few manufacturers able to produce the specialized glasses, and the "OxyIso Colorblindness Correction Medical glasses" are now available commercially on Amazon.com.

The Takeaway*: Many useful inventions did not sell well due to (i) lack of funding or (ii) improper marketing. Finding the right marketer and right manufacturer cannot be taken lightly, for without those two proponents of a project, even a great invention might never see the light of day.*

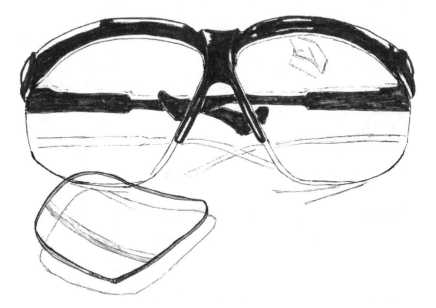

The Fastener

In 1948, a Swiss engineer, *Georges de Mestral* was on a morning hike with his dog in an Alpine forest. They passed through a *burdock* bush and got covered with its *burr* (prickly heads that are noted for clinging onto animal fur and cotton/wool clothing).

Upon returning home, De Mestral inspected one of the many burrs stuck to his pants under his microscope. He noted the small hooks that enabled the seed-bearing burr to cling so strongly to the tiny loops in the fabric of his pants.

De Mestral raised his head from the microscope and smiled, he had been inspired by what he saw to design a two-sided fastener, one side with stiff hooks like the burrs, and the other side with soft loops like the fabric of his pants.

To develop a practical, flexible, and reliable fastener, De Mestral toyed around with several materials, created several surfaces with hooks and loops; then 7 years later after his incident with the burdock burr, in 1955, he settled on nylon as the material for his invention, and patented his design with the name '*Velcro*', derived from two French words: velour & crochet (meaning: velvet fabric & hook)

Ever since then, Velcro rivaled the 'zipper' as the multi-purpose fastener of choice. Today, Velcro is a multi-million dollar industry, making fasteners of various strengths as per the application it is needed for, and used in almost anything that requires quick, flexible, reusable and strong fasteners.

And to think it all started with prickly bush burr clinging to a man's clothes.

The Takeaway*: This is another story of accidental discovery in nature, one that in the hand of an inspired person was converted to a very useful man-made product for human use.*

Any person can become an inventor, you may already be one but you don't know it. If you have ever adapted or modified something for better usability, then you are an inventor, but you might not like to be one, or didn't find support from your peers, approval from your financiers, or quickly gave up on your idea because you didn't believe so much in it.

Had it not been for all those inventors and discoverers who were driven by inspiration to introduce their useful creations throughout history - starting from the discovery of fire, and up to humanoid robots and beyond, humanity wouldn't be what it is today.

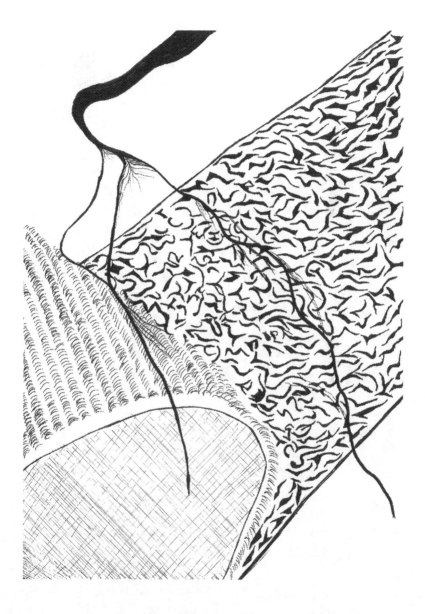

Serious Humor

U.S. President, Ronald Reagan was distinctly famous for his witty communication skills.

In 1985, to break the ice with the Soviet Union's General Secretary, Mikhail Gorbachev, at the start of a very serious meeting, he told him this joke:

"An American and a Soviet were discussing freedom of speech and in which of their respective countries people enjoyed freedom more.

The American said, *"In my country I can go to the White House, walk into the President's Office, pound his desk, and say "Mr. President, I don't like how you are running things in my country!"*

The Russian said, *"I can do that!"*

The American said, *"Really?"*

The Russian said, *"Sure! I can go to the Kremlin, walk into the General Secretary's Office, pound his desk, and say, Mr. General Secretary, I don't like how President Reagan is running the United States!"*

Both Gorbachev and Reagan burst into laughter at this joke; it succeeded in breaking the ice between those two great leaders, and facilitated their discussions on ending decades of tension and cold war between their two countries.

The Takeaway: The fascinating power of humor continues to be a subject of discussion. Although its results can be unpredictable, yet, depending on (i) the readiness of the other party to listen, (ii) the right timing to say it, and (iii) the appropriateness of the joke for the issue at hand, and (iv) who is the person saying it, humor has proven to be very powerful in defusing tense moments.

The next time you face a stressful situation, why don't you test its effectiveness? I repeat, (i) provided that the other party is willing to listen, and that (ii) the moment is appropriate for saying it, (iii) telling the right joke that you can link to the issue at hand, has been known to cool down the tension.

Nails

Source: *Several on the internet*

A little boy had a bad temper.

His father gave him a bag of nails and told him that every time he lost his temper, he must hammer a nail into a fence post in the backyard.

That first day, the boy hammered 37 nails into the fence. Over the next few weeks, as he gradually became more conscious of his unjustified temper and learned how to control it, the number of nails hammered daily gradually lessened; he found it easier to hold his temper than to hammer nails into the fence.

Finally, a day came when the boy did not lose his temper at all. He told his father about it, who although was happy to hear that, suggested that the boy now pull out one nail for each day that he was able to hold his temper.

The days passed and the young boy was finally able to tell his father that all the nails were gone, and took his father to the backyard to show him that there were no more nails in the fence.

The father said, "*You have done well, my son, but look at the many holes it has; this fence will never be the same. When you say things in anger, they leave scars just like these. If you stab a man with a knife then pull it out, it won't matter how many times you say I'm sorry, because the wound will still be there.*"

The Takeaway: If what you say or do can hurt others, choose your words and actions carefully, and assess how they might react to them before you say or do them: If I say or do it this way, they may respond like so; and if I say or do that way, they may respond like so and so.

You may be able to fix the hurt but it will leave a scar, and this they won't forget.

"Talk to people about what they want to hear and they'll stay for more; talk to them about what you want them to hear and they'll soon turn away." - Nabil N. Jamal

Tribal Cleansing

Source: *The Internet*

I have recently come upon this truly wonderful, old African tribal tradition.

It is said that in this tribe when someone does something wrong or cruel, they would take him to the center of their village, and every one would sit in a circle around him for two days and remind him of all the good thing that he's done in his life.

The tribe believes that every person is born good, but that they would sometimes make mistakes, and the community sees those bad deeds as cries for help.

They would band together for the sake of their fellow man to help him reconnect with his true good nature - until he remembers all the goodness within.

The Takeaway: *Although the name of this tribe was withheld online, it remains a great story of solidarity and team spirit, that work together to cleanse and forgive someone we care about.*

Flight of Wild Geese

Natural Scientific Observation

1. Wild geese fly in a **V**-shape formation. The average speed of the flock is *71%* faster than the average speed of an individual goose.

   Lesson: People united by a common goal, achieve that goal much faster and easier because they benefit from their joint effort.

2. If a goose gets out of the formation, it instantly feels the drop in its flight speed; so it immediately returns to the formation to gain its speed.

Lesson: If we had sense like geese, we would stay in the formation of those with our same direction; they offer us their direction and support, as we could too.

3. The rear geese cry out to <u>encourage</u> the lead goose to maintain the speed of the formation.

Lesson: Team members who are not leaders, should not cry out to criticize and demoralize those who are, rather their cries must be to encourage their leadership to keep up the good work for the entire team's benefit.

4. When the lead goose feels tired, it retreats to the rear of the formation to allow another goose take the lead. This way, the speed of the flock does not slow down.

Lesson: Always have a replacement (person) ready to replace the leader when he needs a break; the ongoing operation should not stop if the original leader is away.

5. When a goose gets sick or shot and falls down, two (2) geese leave the formation and follow her to help and protect her, and they stay with her until she is

able to fly again or dies. They then continue their voyage with another passing flock or seek out their old one.

Lesson: If we had sense like geese, we would support each other in our moments of difficulty, exactly as in our moments of strength.

Curious Camel

Source: *The internet*

A young camel asked his mother, *"Why do we have humps?"*

She answered, *"As you know, son, we live in the desert where water is scarce. To survive without water for long periods, we store water in our humps."*

He then asked, *"Ok, why are our legs long and our feet rounded?"*

She answered, *"Son, they help us walk in the desert better than anyone else."*

He continued, *"And why are our eyelashes long and thick? They sometimes bother my sight."*

She replied, *"My son, those long, thick eyelashes protect your eyes from the desert sand and hot wind."*

The son then summed up, *"So the hump is to store water which we can use to survive in the desert, the legs and feet are for walking better than others through the desert, and these long, thick eyelashes protect our eyes from the desert sand and hot wind."*

The Takeaway: *To let your audience accept your answers and remarks, let them visualize it - see the benefit or a clear meaning in it. By giving it a visual that they can associate with, they will more readily accept it.*

Train Tracks

I always use this story as a *decision-making scenario* in my performance development training sessions.

Here is the scenario; will you decide correctly?

The scenario takes place in the train station of a town in a third world country.

Six children are playing on an active rail track (and they know it is active), and one child is playing alone on a disabled rail track (and he knows it is disabled), and you are the station master standing quite a distance away from them, but close to a manual rail track switch.

Suddenly a train approaches on the active rail track, but it is not destined to stop in this town, it will not reduce its speed, it will keep going. You shout to the six children to get off the active rail track, but they don't react.

You do not have much time to think. Will you hit the manual rail track switch and shift the train to the disabled rail track - towards that single child, or will you let it continue on the active rail track where the six children are playing?

You must DECIDE now! Please take a *decision* before you proceed any further. Thank you.

The Takeaway: *This is not an easy decision because of its gravity and because it has to be taken instantly.*

Many readers will opt to sacrificing one child to save six. But, is this a sound decision? Will it occur to them that this single child is deliberately playing on the disabled rail track to avoid the risk of death, and yet, they are considering sacrificing him for the sake of the others who are dangerously playing on the active rail track?

We face such challenges every day, in our work, at home, with friends, and society; and usually, the minority is sacrificed for the sake of the majority, even if the majority is acting carelessly.

The right decision is not to change the path of the train, because:

1) *As the six children know they are playing on the active rail track, they will move as soon as the train gets near them. Certainly these children are playing on the train track every day, and they do move off the track as a train approaches.*

2) *But if you change the path of the train, the child playing on the disabled rail track will not move from his place when he hears the train approaching, because he is believes he is in a safe area. This child will surely be killed.*

3) *The second rail track might have been disabled for a good reason; it might be damaged or a dead end, we don't know . . . , but switching the path of the train to save the lives of six children, might end up with the derailing of the train off the track, and the death of hundreds of passengers on the train plus that one child.*

And although we take many right decisions every day, we must admit that hasty decisions, taken on the spur of the moment, are often wrong. We all make mistakes and that is why we have erasers on pencils!

How did you decide, did you switch the train to the disabled track?

In my performance development training sessions, I have tested this same scenario on a population of around 1,483 front-liners, and separately, on their 223 immediate managers and supervisors; and their results were as follows:

Decision Making Scenario	Right Decision	Wrong Decision
Front-Liners	58%	42%
Managers and Supervisors	9%	91%

Amazingly, front-liners (sales, service, reception, etc.) who interact with clients more frequently than their management, have made more sound decisions; I tend to believe that because their jobs demand their handling client situations more frequently than their immediate managers do, that the experience they accumulate over time, makes them think "bottom-line" and take better decisions under pressure.

Weight of a Glass of Water

Source: The internet

A university teacher began his class by holding up a glass of water for all to see, and asked the students, *"How much do you think this glass of water weighs, 50ml, 100ml, 150ml . . . ?"*

The students gave various answers.

"I really won't know unless I weigh it," said the teacher, *"but what would happen if I held it up like this for a few minutes?"*

"Nothing", several students replied.

"Ok, what would happen if I held it up like this for an hour?, the teacher asked.

"Your arm would begin to ache", said one of the students.

"You're right, now what would happen if I held it like this all day?"

"Your arm could go numb, you might have severe muscular stress and pain, and may need to go to hospital", ventured another student.

"Very good", said the teacher, *"but during all this, did the weight of the glass change?"*

"No", was the unanimous answer.

"Then what caused my arm ache and the muscle stress?" asked the teacher.

The students were quiet.

"What should I do now to stop the pain?" asked teacher.

"Put the glass down!" said one of the students.

"Exactly!" said the teacher, *"Life's problems are something like this; hold them for a few minutes in your head and they seem OK; think about them for a longer time and they begin to ache; hold them even longer and they begin to cloud your thoughts, and you will no longer be able to do anything about them."*

The Takeaway: *It is important to think of ways to tackle the challenges or problems in your life; but what's even more important is to put them down . . . put the glass down, and rest <u>whenever</u> possible. After you have de-stressed, you regain clarity of mind that lets you conceive simple solutions for those matters at hand.*

Golf Ball in Bag

Source: *The internet*

It was the 16th hole in the annual local golf championship, and the tall, handsome newcomer had an excellent chance of winning.

His great shot fell just short of the green, giving him a good chance for a birdie.

Smiling broadly, he strode down the fairway only to stop in dismay; his ball had rolled into a small paper bag carelessly tossed on the ground by someone in the crowd.

If he removed the ball from the bag, it would cost him a penalty stroke. If he tried to hit the ball and the bag, he would lose control over the shot; what should he do?

When I present this dilemma for brainstorming in my performance development training sessions, my trainees would propose several approaches to *getting the ball out of the bag.*

What really happened was that someone in the crowd yelled to the player to burn the paper bag, thus taking the bag out of the equation and totally exposing the ball for a clear shot.

The player did burn the bag and got his clear shot.

The Takeaway: By (i) identifying all parts of a problem, and (ii) not considering the typical approach, but rather (iii) thinking creatively - out of the box, that we become more able to find solutions that no one's ever thought of.

Princess or Talking Frog?

Source: *The internet. Ed Brodov is a negotiation skills specialist, author, speaker, and praised by many as the highest authority on negotiation.*

In one of his seminars, Ed was speaking about what he called *"The Strategy of the Other"* in which he mentioned a tale involving his uncle Willy, who lived to the age of 95 in a very rural area in upstate New York.

The story goes that while Uncle Willy was taking a walk in the park one day, he came upon a talking frog, who told him, *"Hey old man, if you give me a kiss, I'll turn into a beautiful princess."*

Uncle Willy didn't say a word; he picked up the frog, stuck it into his coat pocket and kept on walking.

Half a mile down the road, the frog popped its head out of the pocket and says, *"Hey old man, what about that kiss; remember, I'll turn into a beautiful princess?"*

To which Uncle Willy replied, *"You know, I've been thinking about that, and frankly at my old age, I'd rather have a talking frog!"*

The Takeaway*: Ed's point in this story is that we need to look at a negotiation - not from our point of view - but from the other person's point of view; so while for us it might be a beautiful princess, for the other negotiator it might be a talking frog. Always look at situations from the other person's point of view.*

Because most people tend to see things only from their own point of view, that we have serious conflicts, deadlocks, indecision and delays. Identifying the needs of the other party involved in the negotiation can help us reach a "common ground" solution that accommodates both, theirs and our needs.

"In a negotiation, we must find a solution that pleases everyone, because no one accepts that they must lose and that the other must win . . . Both _must_ win!" - Nabil N. Jamal

Choice of Words

Source: *Taken from a video circulating on the Web.*

An old blind man was sitting on a *busy* street corner in the rush-hour begging for money. Next to his empty tin cup, the following was written on a piece of cardboard: *"Blind - Please help"*; but no-one was giving him any money.

A young advertising copywriter walked past him and read the blind man's sign and saw his empty cup; she also noted how people passed by totally indifferent.

She took a thick marker-pen from her handbag, turned the cardboard sign around, and wrote a new message on the blank side of the sign, then went on her way.

Immediately, people began putting money into the tin cup.

A few hours later, the advertising copywriter passed by the blind man, who recognized her from her footsteps, and asked her what she had written that made such a big difference for him.

So she read it out for him, *"It's a beautiful day, but I cannot see it."*

The Takeaway: This story illustrates how important our choice of words is when we want to truly connect with and move other people. By rewriting the blind man's message, the copywriter gave it value that - from her experience - would appeal better to others.

The rewritten message did not at all ask for money (although this is the sole purpose behind the blind man squatting in the street with his sign); her choice of words diverted the blind man's quest and moved people to empathize - not with his need for money, but with his inability to see the beautiful day.

Sharing Jewels

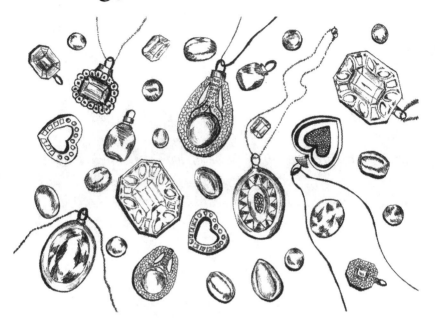

Source: *The internet*

Once there was a very rich and greedy man who loved and hoarded jewels.

One day a friend dropped in for a visit and asked if he could see his collection of jewelry.

So the jewels were brought out, amid much security, and the two men gazed at the wonderful stones.

As the visitor was leaving he said, "*Thank you for sharing your jewels with me.*"

"I didn't give them to you, they belong to Me." exclaimed the rich man.

"Yes of course they are yours," replied the visitor, *"and while we both enjoyed the jewels, the real difference between us is your trouble and expense to buy, worry, and protect them."*

The Takeaway: *You don't need to own something to appreciate its beauty; to some, that something is a "must have", to others it is not. For example: Not everyone likes to own a vintage 1905 car, but everyone appreciates its beauty when it is displayed in public.*

Describing an Elephant

Source: *This is a legendary tale that appears in different cultures - notably the Chinese and Indian, and it dates back over a thousand years.*

Six *blind* men were discussing exactly what they believed an elephant to be, since each had heard how strange that creature was, yet none had ever come upon one before. So the blind men agreed to go to the market together and seek an elephant-owner and discover what the animal is really like; and it didn't take them long to find one in the market.

The first blind man approached the beast and felt the animal's firm flat side. *"It seems to me that the elephant is just like a wall"*, he said to his friends.

The second blind man reached out and touched one of the elephant's tusks. *"No, this is round and smooth and sharp - the elephant is like a spear."*

Intrigued, the third blind man stepped up to the elephant and touched its trunk. *"Well, I can't agree with either of you; I feel a squirming writhing thing - surely the elephant is just like a snake."*

The fourth blind man, who was certainly quite puzzled by now, reached out and felt the elephant's leg. *"You are all talking complete nonsense,"* he said, *"because clearly the elephant is just like a tree."*

The fifth blind man stepped forward and grabbed one of the elephant's ears. *"You must all be mad - an elephant is exactly like a fan."*

The sixth man held the elephant's tail, disagreed, *"It's nothing like any of you described - the elephant is just like a rope."*

And all six blind men continued to argue, based on their own particular experiences, as to what they thought an elephant was like. It was an argument that they were unable to resolve; each of them stressed his own impression of the elephant, and wasn't willing to accept his friends' different impressions; and although each of them was right, none could imagine the whole shape of elephant correctly.

The Takeaway*: There is never just one clear-cut way of looking at a matter - there are always different perspectives, meanings, and perceptions, influenced mainly by what each person is expecting to find.*

We need to find a "common ground of agreement" that accommodates every person's view, because no one is willing to accept other people's views if they are not willing to accept his in return.

The Takeaway of this story reaffirms the Takeaway in the "Princess or Talking Frog" story in this book.

Last Hairs

Source: *The internet*

An old lady looked in the mirror one morning; she had three remaining hairs on her head. Being a positive person, she said, *"I think I'll braid my hair today."* So she braided her three hairs, and had a great day.

Some days later, as she looked in her mirror, she saw that she had lost one hair and that only two were left. *"Two hairs . . . I think I'll have a center-parting today."* She parted her two remaining hairs, and again had a great day.

A week or so later, she saw that she had just one hair left on her head. *"One hair . . . ,"* she thought, *"I know . . . a pony-tail will be perfect."* Again, she had a great day.

A few days later, when she looked in the mirror, that last her had fallen off; she was now completely bald.

"Finally bald," she said to herself, *"how wonderful! Now I won't have to waste time doing my hair anymore."*

The Takeaway: *Although we always hear of its amazing benefits for our well-being, most of us don't bother to adopt it into our way of living. Think positively, make the best of every situation, no matter how ugly it may be, but at least you will not feel so bad about yourself. Now the best part: as a direct reaction, every person with whom you interact, will feel your contagious, positive vibes and reciprocate positively with you; now isn't this much better than everything being negative?*

Salesman and Farmer

Source: *The internet, characters were modified by the author for context appropriateness.*

An agricultural products salesperson arrives at his pre-announced venue in a farming town to introduce farmers to new tools and methods of raising crop in times of water shortage.

He set up his laptop, connected it to the projector, made sure that all seats had the necessary product brochures, and waited for the invited participants to flock in.

An old farmer walked in and took a front seat. It was now time for the presentation to start, but no-one else came, besides this old farmer.

"I'm not sure it's worth proceeding with the presentation. How about I invite you to a hot drink in the coffee shop?" asked the salesman, anticipating a positive reaction from his audience of one.

"Well, I'm just a simple farmer," replied the old man, *"But when I go to feed my sheep, and if I find only one, I surely don't leave it hungry."*

Feeling ashamed at his proposal, the salesman delivered his full, two-hour presentation, finishing with his new lesson that *no matter how small the need, our duty remains*; and thanked the old farmer for the lesson he had just learned.

"Was that okay?" asked the salesman, as he packed his laptop.

"Well I'm just a simple farmer," replied the old man, *"But when I go to feed my sheep, and if I find only one, I surely don't force it to eat what I brought for the whole herd."*

The Takeaway: *Customize. We should tailor what we say or do depending on . . .*

(i) <u>Who</u> the receiver is. Example: You would explain a serious matter to your adult son differently from how you explain it to his 8 year-old brother.

(ii) <u>Needs</u> of the receiver. Example: A mother buying a car cares to have safety and a big trunk that can hold all her supermarket shopping; so you talk to her in those terms. For a man, speed, sound system, GPS, built in communication system are what he looks for in a car; again here, you should tailor your talk to address his needs.

(iii) <u>Size</u> of your audience - what you say or do with one person, may not apply for a big crowd, and vice versa.

(iv) <u>Relevance</u> of the matter to the receiver. Talk to people about what they want to hear so that they'll listen, otherwise, if you talk about something they don't care about, they won't listen.

Rage on the Buddha

One day, as the Buddha (563-483BC), was teaching a group of his disciples, he was subjected to an outpour of insults from an angry spectator.

The Buddha listened patiently while the stranger vented his rage, and then the Buddha spoke, *"If someone gives a gift to another person, who then chooses to decline it, tell me, who would then own the gift? The giver or the person who refuses to accept the gift?"*

"The giver," said the group; *"Any fool can see that,"* added the angry stranger.

"Then it follows, does it not," said the Buddha, *"that whenever a person tries to abuse you, or to unload their anger on you, you can choose to decline or to accept their abuse; you can decide who owns and keeps the bad feelings."*

Everybody, including the angry stranger understood.

The Takeaway: *"No one can make you feel inferior without your consent." - Eleanor Roosevelt*

<u>*Every one*</u> *has the choice whether or not to accept personal intimidation from another person's abuse.*

Now there are various degrees of abuse, I list some here: insults, pressure, harassment, oppression, torture, etc., but the truth remains: no one can take away your freedom of choice in how to handle each of those degrees unless you decide otherwise.

Let us take for example, an extreme case of abuse; a person is imprisoned and tortured to force him to confess to something he knows nothing of. His jailers will increase his torture level until they identify his breaking point, the point at which he is ready to confess to whatever they want so as to temporarily suspend their torture; I say temporarily, because once he does give in to their intimidation, there is no turning back; they now know his breaking point, and they will step up the pain, after all, what's to stop them?

Remember: You always have a choice; no one can intimidate you or break your spirit unless you allow them to.

Sparrow in winter

Source: *the author*

This is one of my favorite stories; I regularly use it in my performance development training sessions, because of the four inherent lessons it provides.

It was the end of Autumn, and time for birds to start migrating to warmer lands; but this sparrow who was enjoying the lovely countryside, decided to stay on as long as possible.

As soon as winter's first raindrops started to fall on its feathers, the sparrow realized it was now time to fly south. As it took off facing strong winds, it also started to snow. The sparrow was unable to fight against the frosty wind, and the weight of the gathering snow on his wings forced him to the ground and soon covered his entire body.

The sparrow broke a hole in the snow with his beak and started to cry out for help.

A dog found the snow-covered bird, but the snow had already hardened around him. The dog was unable to burrow in the mass of snow to free him, so it pooped over it and walked away.

The sparrow thought to itself, *"Adding insult to injury, this dog pooped on me when I am freezing to death, and now I have the horrible smell of the dung on top of it."*

But the dog's warm dung melted all the snow covering the sparrow and hardened, providing a warm casing around the sparrow against the biting wind and snow.

And yet, the sparrow continued its cries for help because it could not bear the stench and the idea of being covered in dung.

A cat now heard the bird's cries and came to inspect the pile of dung. It then proceeded to dig into the hardened dung. The bird thought to itself, *"At last, someone has come to set me free."*

No sooner had the cat uncovered the dung, it grabbed the sparrow and ate it.

The Takeaway:

1. *Do not miss a timely opportunity. Because this sparrow put off migrating south, the window of opportunity passed him by.*

2. *Not everyone who poops on you is your enemy. The dog tried to get the sparrow out, and then it resorted to warming and sheltering it with its dung.*

3. *Not anyone who pulls you out of poop is your friend. The cat dug the sparrow out, not to save him, but to enjoy him as a meal.*

4. *When you're covered with poop, keep your mouth shut. After being covered with the dog's dung, had the sparrow not continued to cry for help, the cat would not have eaten him.*

A Drop of Honey

Source: *Original author unknown presented by Nada Ghalayini.*

A king and his minister were sitting on the palace balcony overlooking the market place. The king was eating honey as he was admiring the magnificent city he ruled.

A little drop of honey spilled from his spoon onto the balcony ledge.

The minister was about to call a servant to wipe up the honey, when the king waved a hand to stop him. *"Don't bother; it's only a little drop of honey."*

The minister watched as the drop of honey dripped from the balcony ledge to the street below.

Soon, a buzzing fly landed on the drop of honey. A nearby lizard shot out its long tongue and caught the fly. A cat leapt on the lizard. A dog pounced on the cat.

A dog-cat fight erupted in the street. The cat's owner was horrified to see her cat being attacked by the dog and started whacking the dog with her broom. The dog's owner was horrified to see his dog being attacked by the cat's owner and started whacking the cat with his stick.

The minister was about to call a guard to go deal with the situation, when the king said *"We shouldn't interfere, it's not our problem."*

Soon, people started coming out from their stalls and houses to see what the screaming and shouting was all about, and joined in the arguments. Very quickly, the arguments became violent and a fight broke out in the street.

The worried minister turned to the King but his only comment was, *"I know what you are thinking, but the police will handle it; besides, it is not our problem."*

The police came and tried to break up the fight, but the people were so angry, each side convinced that they were right, that they started attacking the police.

The fight rapidly became a full scale riot which swiftly escalated into looting and destruction all over the city. Buildings were set on fire, and by nightfall, this magnificent city was reduced to a pile of smoking ashes.

The king and his minister watched all of this happen while still in their seats on the balcony. "*Oh dear, what a shame . . .*" the king said shyly, "*maybe that drop of honey WAS our problem!*"

The Takeaway: *Admitting mistakes early may allow you a chance to fix them while they are still manageable.*

Snake in the Food

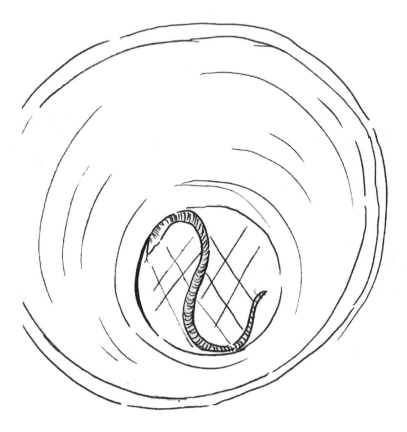

Source: *Unknown author*

A farmer was sent to deliver something to the house of his master - the owner of the land on which he works. His master received him well and offered him a bowl of soup. As the farmer was about to eat it, he noticed that there was a small snake in the bowl, but ate the soup and all its contents without saying a word so as not to show disrespect for his master.

A few days later he started having abdominal pains which necessitated his visiting his master again to acquire medication. The master asked him what he felt and brought him what he thought was the appropriate medication with a glass of water to wash it down his throat.

As the farmer was about to swallow his medication he noticed a small snake in his glass of water, and decided not to be quiet about it this time; so he shouted loudly that his sickness was originally from the snake that was in the food of his last visit.

The master laughed loud and pointed to the ceiling from which a big "S"-shaped wooden arch was hanging. He told the farmer that what he saw in his bowl and glass was a mirror reflection of the arch in the ceiling and not a real snake.

The farmer looked inside his glass again and realized that what his master had said was true, what he now saw was the reflection of the wooden arch and not a snake at all. The farmer then apologized to his master and left his house without even taking the medicine. He instantly regained his health.

The Takeaway: Fear manifests itself negatively in human behavior.

1. *We tend to accept things that we know or feel are wrong. The farmer ate the snake that he imagined out of courtesy to his master; he shouldn't have ignored what he imagined in the first place.*

2. *Trusting and timid people tend to swallow whatever they are given. This is especially valid of those who follow any leader whose agenda does not consider their welfare.*

3. *There are times when our emotions fool us into believing that some things are not quite right; one should take a second look at the matter before forming a quick opinion; when the non-existence of the snake was made clear to the farmer, he saw matters differently.*

The Fox and the Sick Lion

by *Aesop*

It was reported that the lion became sick and confined to his den, where he would be happy to receive anyone who would come to pay him a visit. All the beasts accordingly visited, except the fox who observed from afar and kept away. The lion noticed this and sent the jackal to the fox to tell him that he was expected to visit like all the rest.

The fox told the jackal to pass his sincerest reverence to his master, and to say that he had more than once approached the den to visit, but that he had observed all visitors' foot prints pointed into the den and none outwards; and not being satisfied with that, he decided to stay away.

(The lion had been eating all his visitors.)

The Takeaway: *"It is wise to consider a matter carefully before jumping in carelessly."*

-Nabil N. Jamal

Naming a Great Dish

One day in ancient China, a farmer who lived in a grass hut was out in the field when, for some reason, his hut caught fire just as a pig happened to be running through it (in ancient China, pigs roamed free). The pig got burnt to death inside the hut.

Upon returning, the farmer was devastated at the loss of his hut, and proceeded to remove the burnt carcass of the pig, which left sticky liquids on his hands. As he licked his fingers to clean them, he discovered they had a very nice taste.

So he cut a slice from the pig's loin and tasted it, it was delicious. He then called all his neighbors to come taste this roast pig, and everybody loved it. This is how the famous Chinese dish 'roast suckling pig' was accidentally discovered and named after the farmer *suckled* on his fingers.

To repeat this delicious meal, farmers would repeat this incident - place a pig in a grass hut and burn the hut down, until many years later, when someone brought the idea of roasting on a rotating skewer from Turkey, and suggested roasting the pig on a skewer.

The Takeaway*: Many people advocate that if traditional methods get the job done, why change them? Why reinvent the wheel? But the truth of the matter is that today, just like the fact that you no longer need to burn a hut down to roast a pig, we must embrace new, much more efficient and cost-effective techniques that can save time and money.*

The difficulty lies in identifying if the new methods are truly beneficial or not.

Fun Can Change Behavior

www.thefuntheory.com is a website dedicated to the thought that simple, fun ideas can be applied as projects that change people's behavior for the better.

For example to encourage people to take the stairs instead of the escalator at an underground train station, *thefuntheory.com* team covered the stairs with a giant piano keyboard (*that really works*), such that if people took the stairs, their steps played musical notes. This has encouraged many people to take the stairs instead of the escalator - simply because it is fun.

In another example, *thefuntheory.com* team placed a sound device inside a public park waste bin that would play a fun sound of "*falling into a deep well*" whenever people disposed of their litter in it. Before installing this device, most people would throw/leave their litter on the park grounds; after installing it, the litter thrown inside the garbage bin almost *tripled*. Again, people were encouraged in a fun way, to dispose of their litter in the waste bin.

The Takeaway: *The above two examples confirm that people are more ready to change their behavior if we involve them in a fun activity that directly promotes such a change.*

For those conscious of their environment and society, and care to make things nicer for everyone, adopting ideas like those of thefuntheory.com can really help achieve their cause.

A Word of Advice

Source: *the internet*

A man was smoking one cigarette after another at an airport while looking out of a massive window at the movement of airplanes; when a concerned man walked up to him and asked, *"How much do you smoke in a day?"*

The smoker: *"Why are you asking such a question?"*

The concerned man: *"Well, if you had collected that money instead of smoking, that plane in front of you, would have possibly been yours by now."*

The smoker: *"Do you smoke?"*

The concerned man: *"No".*

The smoker: *"Does that plane belong to you?"*

The concerned man: *"No."*

The smoker: *"Thanks for your kind advice, but that plane does actually belong to me, so keep your advice to yourself."*

The smoker was an Indian industrialist whose interests included an Airline.

The Takeaway: Not every good advice hits; it may lose its intended usefulness if we emphasize its possible gain or loss beyond logical proportion, thus giving the hesitant receiver an excuse to refute it.

Days to Rescue

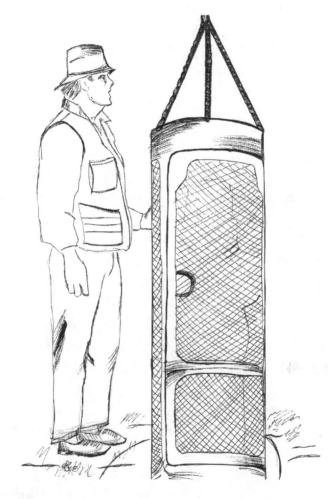

Source: BBC World News

On Aug. 5, 2010, thirty three (33) Chilean miners were trapped inside a very deep gold and copper mine, when a portion of the mine collapsed, locking them 2,300 feet in an underground shelter.

17 days later, on Aug. 23, the rescue team had successfully bored a narrow vertical shaft to the underground shelter looking for possible survivors. The trapped miners attached a note to the drill bit as it was being withdrawn, announcing to the world that they were still alive.

The overjoyed President of Chile, Sebastian Piñera read the note on TV, "*The 33 of us in the shelter are well!*", he added, "*It might take months to get the trapped men out, but it doesn't matter how long it takes, what matters is to have a happy ending.*"

Food, hydration gels, and a walkie-talkie were lowered to the trapped miners through the narrow shaft.

Finally, after 69 days, the rescue team had successfully widened the shaft to fit a cylindrical rescue capsule, and one by one, the miners were a*ll pulled out.*

The Takeaway*: In order to think clearly in situations of high pressure, we must remember to control our fears and maintain hope for a solution.*

It took 17 days for the rescuers just to discover that there were survivors deep inside the mine; this is quite a long time. Had they "given up" on finding survivors before then, those miners would have surely been taken for dead, and that would have ended the rescue operation.

But it was the media's presence that made it a national involvement, as well as the highly-publicized President's personal statement of hope, that made both, rescuers and survivors believe that all efforts will eventually succeed.

"Never, Never, Never, Never Give-up." - Winston Churchill

Brainwashed Not to Think

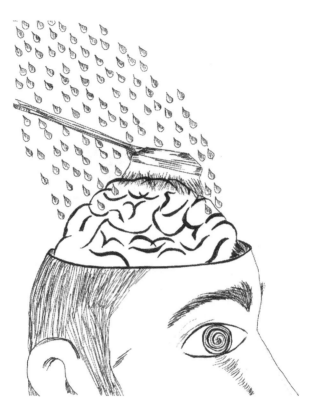

Source: *online research from several sources.*

Can you answer the following riddle in one 7-letter word?

_ _ _ _ _ _ _ preceded God.
The dead have _ _ _ _ _ _ _ to lose.
Wealthy People need _ _ _ _ _ _ _.
_ _ _ _ _ _ is impossible.
If you eat _ _ _ _ _ _ _, you will die.

For those of you who do not wish to bother thinking of the answer, you will find it at the end of this story.

80% of Kindergarten children got this riddle right, but only 5% of Stanford University graduates figured it out! How come?

Over a period of over fifty years, the *'Torrance Tests of Creative Thinking'* have concluded the following two relationships between age and creative thinking:

1. *As people get older, their creative thinking diminishes.*

   That is, a 5-year-old child is much more creative than a 15 year-old teenager, who in turn is much more creative than a 25-year-old adult. This statement correlates with the findings of the above riddle.

   Research has shown that from the day we are born and until age 18, we are subjected to no less than 184,000 external negative influences that limit our thinking process. Hearing such words as: *'no'* - *'don't'* - *'you can't'* - *'it cannot be done'* - *'it's ugly'* - *'you're stupid'* - *'you're doing it wrong'*, etc., so many times, tends to limit our exploration of possibilities and our creativity, and it also brainwashes us with what we are allowed to think and do only.

   The Torrance Tests also found that as the control group of children who were exposed to <u>minimal</u> negative influences became adults, they showed a lot more creativity to explore and think uninfluenced - than any other person.

This proves that by being *Subjected to the Negative Influence of Other People, (which Zig Ziglar coined as SNIOP)* from childhood to age 18, causes us to be less creative as adults.

Observation-2: Child creativity is diminishing very significantly over time.

That is, a 5-year old child in 1980 was much more creative than a 5-year-old child in 2010.

Why are we witnessing this regression in human creativity? The answer is both logical and sad:

a) In the past, children would go into the backyard and have fun playing hide and seek, basketball, football, riding a bike, and climbing a tree, . . . , all, physical activities.

b) In today's computer age, urban city homes no longer have backyards, one reason why urban children stay indoors, *'seated'*, with their eyes, like those of an adult, glued to a computer or smart phone screen, playing electronic games, watching movies, or chatting on digital social media. They no longer bother to do things with their hands, like playing with Lego blocks, assembling a model airplane, or exploring the outdoors, because they believe that everything, anything they want to see or do is readily available online.

This endorses Torrance Tests' second finding, that the more modern our lives become, the less self-reliant we become, and the less creative.

The Takeaway: Apart from the above observations, it is unfortunate that high schools today decide on the university specialization of their students - based on (i) their test results in the last couple of years in high school, and (ii) the ever-changing specialized employment needs. Freedom of choice in higher education is fast becoming a thing of the past; you must specialize in the new job needs, what the market needs, or no place for you in the university.

I herein predict, because we have so frequent changes in specialized job needs in our fast-paced times, and by the time that university students graduate to fit those job needs, that those needs would have again changed; and so, fresh graduates would face certain unemployment.

Brainwashed not to think! Where is it going to lead us?

The answer to the riddle at the beginning of this article is the word: 'nothing'

A Shoe That Made a Difference

Source: *The internet*

The 1954 Football World Cup is best known to all Germans as the *"Miracle of Bern"* for a very good reason; crushed and split after World War II, West Germany had more pressing issues to deal with than a football match in Switzerland; but in the end, it was exactly what the country needed.

Hungary was expected to win the tournament. In the five years prior to the World Cup 1954, Hungary had remained unbeaten in 32 games, and was also the reigning Olympic Champion and winner of the Central European International Cup in 1953.

Victory seemed out of reach for West Germany; Hungary and West Germany had already met in the group stage, with Hungary winning 8-3.

It was forecasted that there will be heavy rain that day. West Germany' coach, *Sepp Herberger*, was worried that his players would slip and slide on the wet, muddy field and not be able to manoeuver and take accurate shots. So he phoned his close friend, *Adi Dassler*, owner of a small sports shoes factory in West Germany, just *one* day before the Final, and described the problem to him, adding that he quickly needed a miracle shoe that can overcome those obstacles, and that Adi should urgently manufacture them for his players to wear in the Final - *in one day*.

Adi dropped everything; this was a very important and decisive event. German national pride was at stake.

The new shoes that Adi made had thinner, lighter leather and bigger screw-in studs on the bottom.

Adi finished the order and arrived at the Final in Bern during the first half of the match. As Herberger expected, both the Hungarian and the West German teams were slipping and sliding on the muddy field, struggling with rain-soaked boots with studs that were too short to find a grip in the mud.

The score was: 2-0 in favor of Hungary.

The West German team changed their shoes for the second half of the match, and went on to score 3 goals and winning with more grip and a better feel for the ball.

For the Germans, the victory brought a much-needed confidence that their country is once again standing tall after its humiliating defeat in World War II.

For Adi Dassler, his innovative football shoes brought instant international recognition to his professional sports brand *"adi.das"* and market leadership for the Football World Cup and the Olympics.

The Takeaway:

a) *When you have a problem that demands external help, consult those whose business it is to solve such a problem; Herbeger consulted with Dassler.*

b) *When you do your very best in a very demanding situation, and succeed in solving a vital problem for others, your efforts will be highly rewarded; because West Germany won, Adidas acquired world fame.*

Phone Call

A small boy went into a grocery shop, headed straight to the phone booth, and dialed a number. The shopkeeper listened to the boy's conversation.

Boy: *"Lady, Can you give me the job of cutting your lawn?"*

Woman (at the other end of the phone line): *"I already have someone doing that for me."*

Boy: *"Lady, I will cut your lawn for half the price of that person who cuts your lawn now."*

Woman: *"I'm very satisfied with the person who is presently cutting my lawn."*

Boy: (with more perseverance) *"Lady, "I'll even clean your patio and sidewalk in front of your home for free, your garden will be the most beautiful garden in town."*

Woman: *"No, thank you."*

The boy smiled and closed the phone.

The shopkeeper, who was listening, walked over to the boy and said: *"Son, I like your attitude; I like that positive spirit and would like to offer you a job in my shop."*

Boy: *"No thanks."*

Shopkeeper: *"But you were really pleading for a job."*

The little boy replied, *"Thank you Sir for your kind offer, I was just checking on my performance at the job I already have; I am the one who is working for that lady I was talking to!"*

The Takeaway: *To maintain a high level of our customers' satisfaction, and ensure our continuing to work for them, it is important - from time to time - to ask what they think about our performance.*

Hands

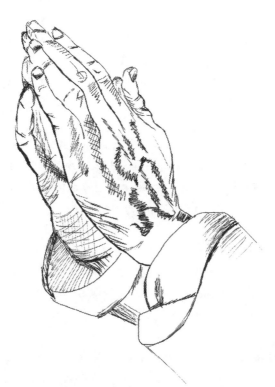

Source: *The internet*

At the dawn of the 16th Century, two young struggling artists, *Albrecht Durer* and *Franz Knigstein*, worked to support themselves while they studied art. But their work consumed so much of their time that their advancement in art was slow; so they made a pact that Durer would go on to study art first while Franz worked at hard labor to support him, and that when Durer was successful, it would be his turn to support Knigstein to resume his art studies.

Durer became successful and attained great fame. When he went back to his town to tell Knigstein, he discovered the enormous price his friend had paid; hard labor had made his fingers twisted that he could no longer make the delicate brush strokes that fine art demanded; nevertheless, Durer kept his promise and supported Knigstein until his death.

One day as Durer was visiting Knigstein, he saw him kneeling with his gnarled hands in prayer. Durer quietly sketched Knigstein's praying hands, and later completed his greatest masterpiece, *"Praying Hands."*

Today, all of Durer's works are exhibited in the top art galleries of the world and in private collections, but none of them holds a place in the hearts of people as "Praying Hands" does.

The Takeaway: *This painting is considered very special because of its delicate depiction of the most noble act of any religion, prayer; and also because of the moving story behind it - that of sacrifice, labor, appreciation, honor, commitment and love.*

Unfinished

By the author

History is full of unfinished works; here are two real stories and the reasons why they were not completed.

Story 1 - *Mark Twain*, author of the great American novels, *Adventures of Tom Sawyer* and *Adventures of Huckleberry Finn*, the latter some call "the Great American Novel", spent 20 years writing *three* versions of *The Mysterious Stranger* but never got around to finishing any of them. Why? Writer's block; Twain was unable to visualize the best ending that would make this a great novel, until he died.

Story 2 - When the foundation stone of Germany's Catholic *Kölner Dom* (*Cologne Cathedral*) was laid in 1248, a legend arose: *If it were to be completed, the world would end.*

Construction was halted in 1473 leaving it *unfinished for **632** years*. Why was it stopped for so long? The curators of the cathedral gave three reasons:

a) In 1438, the Plague, better known as the Black Death had struck Europe, killing an estimated 40-60% of its population; this effectively hindered the Cathedral's construction works.

b) The aftermath of the Plague created a series of religious, social, and economic upheavals, which had profound effects on the course of European history. The Protestant - Catholic War and the Reformation of the Catholic Church, a period that threatened the survival of Catholicism, rendering the completion of this cathedral no longer a priority. It took over 150 years for Europe's population to recover from the Plague.

c) Then one of the cathedral's façade towers was not constructed for 300 years because the original architectural plan for its base was lost.

Only after the lucky discovery of the original plan for the façade in the early 19th Century, and the intervention of the culturally minded Protestant Prussian King Friedrich Wilhelm IV who saw this as a means to improve relations with the large number of Catholic subjects, was the construction resumed and completed by 1880.

The Takeaway: *Even if reasons beyond our control justify our leaving important work incomplete, we need to overcome our own reasons for delaying any further, and diligently put serious effort to complete what we started before it becomes forever marked as an unfinished work. Do your best to finish whatever you started; you must have closure.*

Recognizing the Originator

Source: *The Internet*

The great Italian music composer, *Giacomo Puccini* died in 1924 leaving his final Opera *Turandot*, unfinished.

In 1925, a little known Italian composer, *Franco Alfano*, completed it based on the Puccini's sketches of the Opera ending; and it was premiered (*played for the first time*) on

April 25, 1926 in La Scala Theatre in Milano, conducted by the great, *Arturo Toscanini.*

During the Final Act, Toscanini stopped, the orchestra stopped, Toscanini laid down his baton, turned to the audience and said, *"Here the Opera ends because at this point the maestro died."*

The Takeaway: *The originator of any work gets all the credit, not those who add color to it.*

Although many artists have performed The Beatles' song, 'Yesterday' in different styles, we will always recognize it as a Beatles' song. The same concept must have crossed Toscanini's mind when he honored the originator of Turandot by stopping the performance at the point where Puccini left it unfinished.

Loss of a Thumb

Source: *The internet*

In the mid nineteenth century (1850s), European colonial interests, with the help of religious missionaries, began their deep penetration of the African continent. They would usually break the ice with the tribes they visited by handing out gifts, such as a flintlock hunting rifle to the chief, and a mirror to his wife; and of course, the bigger the tribe, the more the gifts.

In one of the smaller tribes, the chief had a very close friend, who always saw the positive in everything; the chief charged him with the loading of his new hunting rifle with gunpowder and ball-shot, and to be his gun-bearer whenever they go hunting with it.

One day, his friend suggested they fill it with more gunpowder and two ball-shots so as to hunt an elephant with it. When the chief pulled the trigger to shoot, the ignition chamber exploded (because it was blocked with the 2 ball shots), resulting in the chief losing his thumb, and the rifle destroyed.

The chief was in great pain and very angry for losing his thumb and hunting rifle. His friend tried to calm him by saying, *"Thank God that you did not lose all of your hand, or your eye."* This enraged the chief even more, and ordered the imprisonment of his friend in a hut at the edge of the Serengeti desert, and to have him guarded by one warrior.

When his wound healed, the chief returned to hunting with spears. Then one day, as he and his warriors were hunting, they were attacked by a bigger and stronger tribe, who had many rifles. All the chief's men were killed in the brief battle, and he was arrested and taken to their chief.

The victorious chief ordered the immediate execution of the defeated chief so he can annex his tribe, women, children, goats and land.

Now at that time, most African tribes believed that if you hurt a feeble-minded person or someone whose body is incomplete, you will have bad luck.

When the victorious chief saw that that the defeated chief had a missing thumb, he ordered his immediate release. The defeated chief was now without a home to return to; but he remembered he had imprisoned his best friend in a hut at the edge of the Serengeti. He immediately proceeded to release him, apologized for his harsh punishment, and explained how he had survived certain death just because he had a missing thumb.

His friend smiled, and thanked his chief for imprisoning him.

The chief was taken aback with his friend's response, and asked, *"How could you thank me for imprisoning you?"*

His friend replied, *"Because had I been with you and not killed with the rest of our tribe's warriors, then presented with you to the victorious chief, you would have been released because of your missing thumb, and I would have been instantly executed. I would not be alive today had you not imprisoned me in this hut"*.

The Takeaway*: Always look at difficulties from a positive point of view, it may be much simpler/easier to deal with than you imagined, and if you look closely enough, you might find a benefit in every difficulty. Always think before you judge.*

A King is Born

Source: Aesop's Fables

A lioness gave birth to a male cub. All the beasts came to congratulate her on her delivery. One of her visitors, a vixen exclaimed, *"What, only one cub? We vixens have as many as ten at once."*

The lioness smiled and answered her visitor in a dignified manner, *"Yes, only one, but that one, is a Lion!"*

The Takeaway: *In the end, it is quality that really counts not quantity.*

"Like in the zoo, you'll always find lots of monkeys but very few lions." - Nabil N. Jamal

Cookies

Source: *the internet, slightly modified by the author.*

A young woman arrives at the airport a bit early for her flight; she completes her checking in, goes to the shop in the lobby, buys a magazine and a packet of chocolate chip cookies, then heads to the VIP lounge to spend time reading her magazine and enjoying her cookies. Next to the armchair where the packet of cookies lay, a young man sat in the next armchair working on his laptop.

For every cookie that she took from the packet, the young man would also take one - from the same packet. This annoyed her; *how dare he,* she thought, *those are my cookies*; but she maintained her composure.

When they reached the last cookie, the young man took it out of the packet, split it in two and offered her a half. This was too much; *"What a nerve!",* she said staring him in the eye, *"You take my last cookie and offer me half?"* She stood up, shoved her magazine in her bag, stormed out of the room, and headed towards the boarding lounge.

When she eventually sat in her seat in the plane, she pulled out her magazine from her bag only to find her full packet of cookies in the bag, unopened.

It was then that she realized that she had been wrong about the young man and his intentions; it was his chocolate chip cookies that they were eating from in the VIP lounge, not hers; and he was generous to offer her half of his last one. She felt very ashamed about her thoughts as it was now too late to rectify her attitude and apologize to the young man for eating his cookies, for raising her voice at him, and for storming out of the lounge in the manner she did.

"It is always better to look at a matter positively before ruling negatively on it." - Nabil N. Jamal

The Takeaway: *The following quote by Deanna Wadsworth says it all: "Four things you can't recover: The stone after the throw, the word after it's said, the occasion after it's missed, and time after it's gone.", and to which I add one of my own for this story, ". . . you can't recover a hasty judgment after the hurt's been done".*

Last to Surrender

Sources: various from the internet

When Japan surrendered in 1945, Japanese *'holdouts'* - soldiers of Imperial Japan continued to hide in jungles and islands until the 1970s, believing that World War II was still being fought. They had been ordered to fight on to eventual victory or an honorable death; to them, surrender was out of question.

51-year-old, Second Lieutenant *Hiroo Onoda*, his uniform patched and darned, was the last recorded Japanese holdout - a living relic of a war that had ended 30 years before. The last thing his commander had said to Onoda on the island of Lubang, Philippines was, *'Whatever happens, we'll come back for you.'*

Onoda led a small team of Japanese soldiers into the island's jungle and waged a long and aggressive guerrilla campaign over 30 years.

In 1952. the Philippine and Japanese governments made an attempt to capture Onoda's group. They dropped letters and photographs from their families over the jungle; but Onoda's group thinking it was an American ploy to make them surrender, continued to raid local settlements for supplies, often shooting at local peasants. Their attacks had killed or wounded around 30 Filipinos over the decades.

With time, all members of his group were either killed or died from disease or age, except Onoda who remained active in his raids, until a Japanese student and adventurer, *Norio Suzuki*, set out to find him in 1974.

Camping alone within Onoda's 'territory', he managed to strike up a friendship with him, and persuade him to come to a parley in a jungle clearing to meet with Japanese and Filipino representatives. At that meeting, Onoda stated that he could not surrender unless he receives a direct order from his commander, and went back into hiding.

On 9 March 1974, Suzuki returned with Onoda's old commander, former Major *Taniguchi*, who ordered him to hand over his samurai sword and surrender with honor. Onoda instantly obeyed, handing his sword to Philippines president, Ferdinand Marcos.

On his return to Japan, Onoda became a celebrity. He was different from previous returned holdouts in being an officer who had also not stopped fighting.

The Takeaway:

This remarkable story shows the ability of the human spirit to persist and tolerate great hardships for the sake of beliefs and duty; it also shows how a single person's determination, 'Suzuki', can succeed where governments and armies have failed. Yet, from a mental health perspective, it shows the power of the mind to shut out all messages and signals it does not 'wish' to receive.

Double Dare

Source: *various on the internet.*

Upon completing a highly dangerous tightrope walk over Niagara Falls in strong winds and rain, 'The Great Zumbrati' was met by an enthusiastic supporter, who urged him to make a return trip, this time pushing a wheelbarrow, which the spectator had thoughtfully brought along.

The Great Zumbrati was reluctant, given the terrible weather conditions, but the supporter pressed him, "*You can do it - I know you can,*" he urged.

"*You really believe I can do it?*" asked Zumbrati.

"Yes, definitely you can do it." The supporter flattered.

"*Okay, let's do it.*" said Zumbrati, "*Get in the wheelbarrow!*"

The Takeaway: *Never dare someone to do something unless you are ready to be dared in return.*

Throughout history, certain people sarcastically mock those who achieve greatness because they themselves are incapable of such feats. For those who deserve the glory of achievement, putting those mockers in correct perspective is best; in this story, Zumbrati in turn, dared the mocker back.

Interrupted Metamorphosis

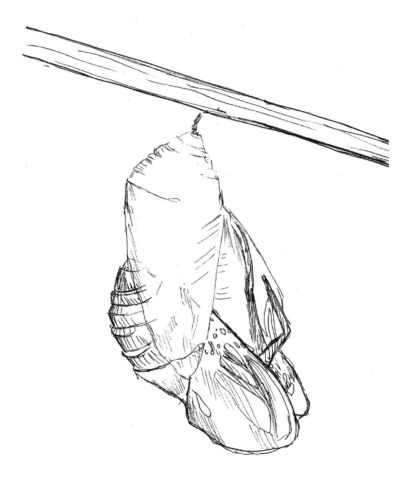

Source: the internet

A man saw a butterfly emerging from a cocoon on a tree twig in front of his house terrace. So he sat for several hours watching it struggle to force its body through the little hole that it punctured in the cocoon. Then suddenly, half way out it seemed to stop making any progress; it appeared stuck.

The man decided to help the butterfly, so he cut open its cocoon. The butterfly then easily emerged, but a strange thing happened, it had a swollen body and withered wings. The man kept watching the butterfly expecting it to take on its correct proportions. But nothing changed. The butterfly stayed the same, and it was never able to fly.

In his kindness to help and his haste to speed up her metamorphosis, the man did not realize that the butterfly's struggle to get through the small opening of the cocoon is nature's way of forcing fluids from the body of the butterfly into its wings so that it would be ready for flight.

The Takeaway: We may need to struggle at times to achieve something, but certainly as always, the experience will make us stronger. When we teach or help others, it is important to realize "when" we must let them do things on their own.